BURNING ALL THE TIME

CHRISTOPHER MURPHY

FIRST EDITION, 2020
Burning All the Time

ISBN 978-1-7323935-9-2

Mongrel Empire Press
Norman, OK
www.mongrelempire.org

This publisher is a proud member of

Versions of some stories appeared earlier in *The Jellyfish Review, Necessary Fiction, BULL, Spartan, Ghost Parachute, The Tulsa Voice* and The Center for Poets and Writers at OSU-Tulsa's *Dear Oklahoma* podcast. Though many of the stories borrow from other writers, one, "A Summer Story" borrows heavily from Hemingway's "A Very Short Story." It was done with intent, but it bears acknowledging.

Created with Vellum

CONTENTS

for my family

BURNING ALL THE TIME

AN ANNUAL REPORT

My annual report, divided by season: Northeastern Oklahoma division.

Fall

§ Children in the swelter of August chilled in agony at Back-to-School advertisements, but on the first day, they delighted in new backpacks and lied about their summers. Many felt the safety of routine combined with the dread of being publicly wrong about everything.

Early reports forecast fewer days at school, concern about politics reaching the children as if politics didn't reach children. Supposedly, Mr. Bryant was sleeping on someone's couch. Some days he barely shaved. Makayla Goingsnake said he couldn't afford gas.

§ Hunting season passed again with no one offering to take me out. In the stand on his property by the scrub of blue dawn, Joe selfied the hunter at repose, bow across his knees, two streaks of camouflage undereye like the Ultimate Warrior. He killed with reverence, ate backstrap in the warmth of his kitchen, and posted his dinner on Instagram. He had rebuffed my subtle hints.

§ The Cherokee National Holiday stickball game at Sequoyah High's football field featured dudes flying ass-over-teakettle. Charlie Mouse, who everyone called Junior, unleashed a barrage on D. He'd barrel to the ball, cradle it between his sticks, and then rain down punishment in high parabolas at the other side's pole.

§ At inside linebacker, Alex Howe led the state in tackles and the Locust Grove Pirates to the 3A Championship, playing through his third concussion of the season. Thirty years later he won't remember where he put his keys, but he'll remember everyone flooding the field as the clock wound down.

§ In the produce section of Reasor's, Becky Jane Fletcher cornered Ann Fite and complained for 15 unbroken minutes about her sprained ankle.

Winter

§ Makayla wore a sweater when she left the house in the postdawn frost, left the sweater inside during lunch because she was literally melting, then forgot the sweater after practice and froze.

§ In the produce section of Reasor's, Becky Jane Fletcher followed Tyler Hodge and asked twice why they didn't get the good clementines.

§ The Tahlequah Christmas Parade beat back for one more year the forces of cynicism and pettiness, debt and fracturing. The Christmas Parade looked backwards in the way Oklahomans do best, with a desire to protect innocence and revel in community. In a document review of related annual reports, the Tahlequah Christmas Parade ranked #55 on the holiday goodwill quotient, outpowering Tucson and Indianapolis.

§ In the cramped singlewide on her parents' property, Jenna Cade chose between heat and presents for her daughters.

§ The holiday season dressed the cities in beauty. There is no locale on the planet—not desert, not cornfield, not jungle, not exurb—that wears the holidays as well as cities. Lights upon lights made a benevolence of glass. Storefronts flaunted in cranberry. I walked arm in arm with Kindra to the *Nutcracker* ballet full of whiskey and champagne. Tulsa glowed like every city of every Christmas of my entire life.

§ An unarmed black man in Tulsa was killed by a cop. The shooting was stricken from her record.

§ Winter, for the third year in a row, was conspicuously brief.

Spring

§ That fucking pollen.

§ Our greatest season, storm season, was an unmitigated victory. 73% of Northeastern Oklahomans reported lying in bed with the blinds tilted open as lightning made a temporary apocalypse of the sky. The rains swept the culverts clean. The space from car to door never short enough. We all got soaked.

§ The avatar of Oklahoman violence, the rage that sits in the blood, the reminder that the earth is cruel and the future uncertain, tornadoes did little damage this year. Patron saint of the forecast, Travis Meyer steered us well. Vian was spared. Tulsa was spared. Stilwell was spared. Miami was spared. Tahlequah's magic held strong. Makayla did not get the chance to sit on her porch, watch the funnel ride the horizon, stick her chin up, and dare it to try.

§ Mostly men, mostly white took to the golf courses to cleanse themselves. We all knew this to be the most manicured, frivolous way to get clean. We all knew what we had to be cleansed of. We took showers afterwards and felt we'd done good work.

§ Cornerstone Fellowship gave Jenna Cade a weekly reason to not drown. Destiny Berry thought they invented hell so the Iron Spoke Free Holiness Church could put her in it.

§ In the produce section of Reasor's, Becky Jane Fletcher didn't know why she was always afraid. Looking at the avocados, she blamed immigrants.

§ As every year, firefly season was a splendor. One night as Kindra and I drove, they rose from the fields by her grandparent's house, an intermittent blanket of light. Across Northeastern Oklahoma, people felt the joy of it, and felt it in the person they loved sitting next to them in a dark car.

§ Seriously, though, the fucking pollen.

Summer

§ Brett spent three days driving posts into his backyard, returning to Lowe's again and again to get the right timber, the right joists, the right crushed angular gravel while his hands ached to cripple. After, the work finished, he drank a beer he could barely hold and surveyed work done right by his own muscle and his own sweat to guard his own tomatoes.

§ The family pooled together, like every year, and bought $2000 worth of fireworks. If you were raised in a nanny state of sparkler-wavers, you looked aghast at nine-year-olds led to mortar tubes by drunken uncles. You heard laughing stories about Granny Rose jumping when a tube tipped over and fired under her lawn chair. In the armor of stale lotion, Bud sweat, and horseshoe dust, you stood gape-mouthed as a raining willow of silver erupted over Papa James' oak.

§ In the produce section of Reasor's, Becky Jane Fletcher raged about Pastor Todd, the state of her asthma, the sugar ants in her kitchen, her nephew on the pills, her broken window unit, Janey Reston's carrot cake, the idiot drivers on 82, and the galdanged heat that drove her mad in a loneliness that haunted her summers since she was a child. She did so at two captive audiences, the first escaping just before the second was backed into the Brussels sprouts. Shopping with her mom, Makayla Goingsnake vowed never to get old.

§ Scissor-tailed flycatchers in gray and orange tumbled in displays of bravado, protection, hunger, and love from the air to alight briefly on the ground, then burst upwards again.

ALL IS DULL AT THE KUM & GO

"IT'S NOT that I let the dog lick it," the woman at the counter with the sling said. "She just gets after it and won't stop."

Past the woman with the sling and the attendant, past Little Debbie and the slushie machines with their twirling faces, Lexi shook the locked beer cooler. Lexi wore a pair of orange basketball shorts and once crushed a boy's pinkie in her fist. Her fake ID said HarleyMarie Turtle, her older sister. I was sleeping over but we'd snuck out after curfew. Lexi was buying beer for us to drink in the little wooden room with the steering wheel at the top of the playground behind her mother's apartment. We'd done it once before and fell asleep yin yang, toe to nose, both grounded later, whatever that meant, Netflix for days.

The Kum & Go was down the street from a 24-hour Dunkin' Donuts. They had iced coffee drinks big enough to fit my whole forearm. I wanted to go there instead. I wanted to sneak back into her mom's apartment with frappucinos and donuts and watch *Supernatural* on Lexi's bed.

She rattled the door again. Her whole family was constantly one step from being pissed. My mom talked about them like adjectives, "They're beyond ornery. You know, they're Turtles." Lexi kept trying to bully the lock. She liked beating the ass off salty bitches who talked out their necks and Stephanie Meyer books but not the movies. I liked being sad and high. She was my muscle and I was her dealer. Also, I'm super smart, which doesn't help at all. I warded off razors and pills with my library card.

"Fucking horseshit. Hey, jackwagon." Lexi waved her hand at the clerk, who had narrow, hairy wrists and terrible skin. He kept looking my way. "Why is this closed?"

"It's two."

Lexi looked at her phone then visibly flexed. I'd seen her whip a girl's mouth in the locker room with a knee brace for saying she had big shoes. The girl, bleeding, had knocked me over and Lexi caught me one-armed. Lexi made me feel fragile.

The clerk said, "It's two a.m. That means no beer." He looked my way.

I saw the bad possibilities spiral out in front of me. Lexi chucking a can of Bang in a frozen line at the clerk's zitty forehead, the clerk innocent like Germans and pipeline workers. Us running out the door, the clerk one-eyed marking Lexi's height. The cops taking me in long enough to put my parents in a bad way moneywise, because we're always that way. Putting Lexi on a raft to the end of her life. She was a Valkyrie. I wanted her to bear hug me between two six-packs and run me safe to the playground behind her drunk mom's apartment whispering 'gay' in my ear. I pinch her arm and said, "Let's go get 60 donuts."

At the counter, the woman with the sling kept talking, "I guess it's healing. I don't know. It feels like it's burning all the time."

A SUMMER STORY

One cool night in Tahlequah, they pushed Liz up to the landing of the bar, the sound of the small creek below. Moths bothered her ears. After a while the overheads dimmed and Christmas lights by the railing went on. Liz could hear everyone downstairs laughing. Rob sat with her. He was hot and still against her shoulder.

He worked the graveyard shift at Love's for the whole semester. When she had her first break, he brought her pizza from work and joked to the silence about gas station food. He got her to sleep wrapped tight in her blanket. After she managed to get up and shower a few nights in a row, he still brought pizza and burritos for her and her roommates. As he walked out to the kitchen to leave them food, she thought of him shirtless in front of the fridge's one light.

Before she left, they looked at each other's phones and chose pictures to post. Her room was hot and silent, and their friends commented and liked their photos. They shared three pictures each, different ones for both of them. None of it was official, but they both felt it was and wanted everyone else to see it.

He texted throughout the summer. She wasn't allowed a phone while working, so she read all his texts on her break and then in the parking lot after work. He said the gas station was terrible. He wondered how she was doing by the river. Once he texted five times in a row that he missed her.

She told him she wasn't going back to school, but she wanted to move to town for him. She would get a job. Her hometown had nothing for her, not the friends who remained, not her mother or stepfather. She visited his apartment. It was hot and damp and smelled like feet. She wasn't sure enough for him and they fought, their first real fight. She kissed him before leaving and texted after, but they still had the fight in them. They both stared at their phones, thumbs paused, mid-text.

She went home. He changed shifts and picked up a second job as a barback at Ned's. The fall teams started their camps. Living in that dry, lonely town, he slept with a tennis player from Belarus. Her strangeness befuddled and thrilled him, a woman from outside the United States. He texted Liz and told her he'd made a mistake and shouldn't have pressed her when she was fragile, even if she didn't feel that way now, and he understood she'd be angry but hoped she'd understand. He thought she was amazing.

The Belarusian's social media showed him, then showed a soccer player from Dallas. He texted Liz late one night and she never responded. She got a job at Dollar General, tried pills and three boys, church and hairdressing, and then other plans though she didn't love any of them.

A BREACH OF CLUB RULES

ROUNDING the top of the second hole, a group jumps in front of Alex and Dave, a breach of club rules. Dave says, "They can't do that," then yells, "Hey! Assholes! You can't do that!"

Dave has survived cancer. He marvels at the rolling beauty of fall, gives frail hugs, always asks after Alex's family in a way that's lonely and touching. Cancer also put blades in Dave's heart. Whether from the chemo or the proximity of death, Dave's fury, his spite erupts and lingers. Immigrant kids are parasites. Muslims a plague. Women are bitches, his ex most of all though he'd still take a turn.

In the past six months, Dave had been hit by a car, broken with pain pills, fired three shots through his backdoor at home-invading teens. Facts are unreliable. He'd been life-flighted after getting hit by the car, which was actually a truck. The kids had helped him move in. He hadn't shot any of them. There isn't much debating the pills. Dave's hands are origami talons.

So, when Dave launches a new volley of "get off the goddamn hole!" Alex is prepared to write it off. Just like he writes off Dave's bottomless litany of jokes, punchlines about reluctant women giving blowjobs, brutal parodies of black men after missed putts. Alex lets it all slide because Alex is a coward who values a quiet day of golf above decency.

Alex tees off while the group, six deep, definitely a breach of club rules, mills around the green. From the top of two, the pastoral spread of Cherokee Trails undulates in variegated browns and bare trees. To the left, the bell at Sequoyah High boops. Far to the right, errant pops come from the firing range. Alex hits a long arcing drive, and the confluence of his body, club and ball makes him a brief conduit for harmony.

On the walk down to their balls, Dave veers onto the third hole where the six gather at the tee box. "Hey, you dickheads. You can't skip around like *fuck*ing *ass*holes." They scramble, deploy. A Sooner red cart buggies up the hill. Alex sighs. He is decades younger than Dave and not crippled by chemo and pill addiction and teens and trucks. On this day, as every day, he is not prepared to throw down over a breach of club rules.

The driver of the Sooner cart reveals himself as the worst sort of chapped ass. He looks like a Rick. He is squat, burly, purple-faced and bellowing with a crimson windbreaker, both windbreaker and cart accessorizing each other in a way that dampens the effect of the man's fury. The other carts establish a front as the Rick launches upright, grabs Dave's lapels and drives him stumbling backwards on his cancer-depleted legs. Dave keeps up the chatter.

Alex experiences a delicious sequential slowing of thought: 1.) Look at this paragon of every surly, pig-eyed, red ass, troglodyte motherfucker of my past five years; 2.) Dave, stop talking; 3.) A fistfight. Over golf; 4.) That gorgeous breeze; 5.) Someone's getting sued.

The Rick puts his hands down and bumps Dave gorilla-style. They bark and bark at each other, but Dave's barking erodes to yapping as he's driven backwards. When Dave hits the ground, the Rick sprawls, hands out, barking spit down at Dave's face. The other five guys stand in an uncertain ring.

Alex says, "Alright, man, enough." The five guys make similar noises, though a few mention Dave's fucking assholes and how it wasn't right, how they'd got cut in front of too. The Rick is up on his hind legs in a rage of Coors breath, explaining to Alex's face what Alex just watched as if Alex hadn't been there. How Dave started it. How the Rick didn't touch him. How Dave shouldn't talk shit if he didn't want his ass beat. Alex, terrified and bored, nods and says, "OK. OK." Rick asks Alex does he want to go too? Dave whimpers on the ground in the fetal position about his back, his back. Because Alex is a coward, though in this instance a better sort of coward, he says, "No, I do not."

A few of the men stay behind and apologize. Both sides are to blame. It's stupid. They're out here to play golf. Alex agrees. At his feet, Dave stays in the fetal position with one hand covering his spine and the other his face. Later, Dave sues. The cancer comes back.

EVERY ACCOMPLISHMENT STARTS WITH THE DECISION TO TRY

JORDAN DYLAN PERRY believed in the inherent goodness of things. He believed it at shows and believed it serving lunch at The Branch and believed it making promotional videos for his new career in realty. He viewed the videos as on-scene reportage of good news.

People had called him pretty since he was a boy. Now he used his face to help, in his little way, make things better. Dylan had a thin beard with a thin mustache that he patted with his fingertips while he was deep on-point.

Tommy Roberts hated Dylan's mustache and Dylan's mustache patting. Jesus Christ, he'd watched Dylan's videos. Tommy finally convinced Dylan by explaining all the ways the bookstore took advantage of the government, the university, and most of all the kids. Dylan had gone through school, Kappa Sig, and feared he might die with his loans.

"So you're saying the bookstore won't punish students by raising prices?" Dylan patted his mustache.

"They have insurance." Tommy looked like Jack White played by a wet squirrel. He made it work in small bursts. He'd been at the bookstore for three years and never had more than a series of lateness and dress warnings. He thought about everyone who deserved to feel a little shittier, mainly Robinson the GM. "No one will even lose their job, except maybe me. The big issue we need to address is after. Have you seen *Goodfellas*?"

Dylan had, but didn't remember.

Tommy turned to Gage, who sat quietly like he sat. "What's your strategy for afterwards?"

Gage sat in front of Ned's fluorescent sign. He drew often from a big carburetor of a vape kit. The vapor smelled like smoke and the sign made it billow red.

"Nothing," Gage said.

"How does that work, nothing?"

"Easy," Gage said. "I don't do nothing like I didn't before. I don't use the bank like I never do. I don't go to work for three days because I'm not scheduled until Tuesday after. I probably don't steal from work for a little while, if that's what you're looking for."

"See, that's what I mean." Tommy slapped his hand into his palm and nodded from Dylan to Gage. "That's a good approach."

"I don't get in any bar fights. I don't cripple anyone. I don't look to topple the government. I don't devise an attack plan like Anders Breivik. I don't make phone videos where I read my manifesto about the climate cooking us all and creeping white genocide and post on one of the Chans. If I made videos about life in Tahlequah, I'd probably keep doing that."

Dylan frowned and cocked his head to the side in the way his mother expressed displeasure. He liked challenging traditional gender roles. "Don't be a shit-giver," he said. "I'm not going for three weeks to surf Costa Rica." Dylan talked to Tommy because Gage made Dylan uneasy, like at any moment he might be fantastically mean.

Gage's part was easy. Gage, in a hoodie, was going to steal Dylan's motorcycle, get a second-hand bike plate from some friends at Junklahoma Salvage east of Tahlequah, use an old motorcycle helmet he had found on Craigslist in Joplin, beat the shit out of Tommy, and take the sack for the bookstore's beginning-of-semester, end-of-week deposit.

Tommy saw it all clear last semester watching Robinson take that whole heavy sack out of the drop safe and hand it to him like it was the affection of a woman. BancFirst was right on the bypass. He'd wait a minute or two, a little bloodied, possibly concussed, go into the bank, no security guard, and say he was robbed. If they saw it, all the better. Dylan would report the missing bike the night before.

They each got a third. Tommy thought it should go 40/40/20 but he didn't say it out loud. He knew from every heist movie that resentment and indulgence were the big reasons everyone got caught. Those two and also bad luck. Tommy hedged against bad luck with rigorous planning. Also the crazy wildcard who fucks things up, but they didn't have one of those.

Dylan considered himself the potential backup getaway driver. He was excellent at long drives. Tommy considered Dylan's sweet stupidity the red herring that would lead the cops astray. He hadn't wanted to include Dylan at all, but one night he got so drunk he maybe mentioned the smallest fragment of the plan, and Dylan, also very drunk but not so drunk he didn't remember the next day, was all about it before his morals kicked in and by then it was too late.

Gage had been easy. He was the only guy Tommy knew sat in the center of a particular Venn diagram: rough looking enough to sell a beating, country enough to reject the concept of authority, and lacking in abstract thought. That's why Tommy was the mastermind—he had the abstract thought to see all the angles before. Gage was the muscle. Dylan, obviously, was the face.

"Obviously," Dylan said, "We probably should make this the last time we get drinks for awhile."

"That's getting the idea. But, here's my thinking. So what? I've had drinks with 20 people on this patio the past month."

"It's a pretty nice plan," Gage said. "Makes a lot of sense long as there's no bad luck. Here's the thing, though. What I can't figure is how y'all going to stop me from taking the money to Kansas or Vegas."

Tommy smiled because that was what he really feared. Before he could answer, Dylan said, "That's easy: anonymous tip. We know who you are. No one will suspect it was us, especially Tommy. He just says that he doesn't know you but for drinking here and I say sorta the same thing. It's easy to believe you overheard about the money drop and robbed him. But why do you want to introduce negativity into the situation? You're creating herd toxicity. It's not necessary."

Gage smiled behind a fat curtain of smoke-smelling vapor. "I'm just full of bull. Here I've gone and soured things. I didn't mean any negativity. It's a fine plan and we'll get it done and be bound for glory. Nobody freestyling. That'll wind you up dead and no one wants that. I'll give you a little love tap, no doubt, but after? All we do is follow the plan. It's like a job, you just do it and you'll be fine. That's the problem. People don't just do their job. They all want something for free. We do this, a simple afternoon's work, and we're off to Valhalla.

"Heck, you don't need to worry about me. I've got only one plan. You'll find me out behind my house afterwards. I'm going to take my third and spread it around. Buy some materials, couple of Lowe's nearby, mom and pop hardware stores those little dead towns headed towards the city. No need to buy any tools even. Like *Goodfellas*, right, buying a new Cadillac? I got my own tools. I'll be out back building something to last. 14-by-14. That'll support a party. Add value to my property. I'm going to watch the fireworks from it. I'm going to drink my black coffee and look out on a pristine new day. Then I'm going to have a big throwdown, all the people who been with me. The right people, good blood. You should come. You got pups, right? Bring them, long as they can handle country dogs. Rotts, Blue Heelers, Pits. Pure-bred mutts. It's a good day coming."

SISTER

SISTER RAN from Tahlequah after Ricky Briggs stood in front of Ned's in his underwear in the rain holding two machetes. He told the cops he was going to kill everyone in the bar. They didn't put much stock in it but circled him, tased him, and restrained him anyways. One cop played ball way back with Ricky and heard Sister tried twice already. The cop told her if she was gonna leave him for real, now was the time.

She hated fake-ass Bentonville. She didn't like Arkansas either. She didn't like Maggie's house or Maggie's husband or, to be honest, Maggie's kids all that much. She liked Maggie's dogs and considered them nephews. To the kids she was 'Sister', just like with Maggie. Maggie said things like "Oh, I just got that at Target" and "My mother's chow chow recipe is lost to time." She was that full of shit.

"You know the rules," Maggie said. She wore what looked like a turban. Sister was in the pool letting the jet blow water between one set of toes, then the other. More than anything, she measured how far Maggie had gotten by her in-ground pool. "All I ask, Sister. Those three."

The Okie came out of Maggie when she hit bottle two of the white wine, when people left the turning lane too slow, when someone put a hand on her kids. The time Uncle Bo, who everyone knew was a piece of shit, shook Maggie's eldest for kicking over his beer on purpose, which Maggie's eldest did do, those kids brats but still kids, and Maggie said,

"Touch my girl again, you fat shit. I'll bust your ass." Everyone across the yard got quiet and Sister laughed and laughed.

Maggie once joked the Okie sure came out of her when Cody Roberts got her pregnant. Maggie said, "He barely made it 30 seconds. He won't even look at me in the hall. Sister, we got to fix it." Sister went with her to the clinic in OKC, though she was serious about church then. That shook her loose just a little, before the drinking did more. She remembered the youth pastor seeing her drunk at Norris Park. "Once you leave what we got," he said, "Nothing'll feel like yes again." He'd been wrong about that.

Maggie pointed at the bruises on Sister's legs and neck and asked, so Sister told her about monkeybites. Ricky liked to take her skin between his knuckles and twist, sometimes in a sexy or funny way, usually not so much. Sister didn't tell her about him putting his hands around her throat, a long time ago in a sexy way but lately, not.

Sister broke rule three when she told Maggie's husband, again, about how Maggie got backstage with Ratt. Her husband did something with Walmart. He said, "the home office" all the time. The one time Maggie took him to a family cookout, her husband said he was from Argentina and Uncle Randy asked if his people got their money from Nazi gold.

Rule three was the smallest rule but Maggie hissed and put her finger up at Sister's face. Still, Maggie, Sister and the girls watched *The Proposal* on the couch and Maggie laughed her old laugh. Like they'd watched *Sixteen Candles* on VHS in their parents' rotten-floor house before a storm dropped a tree on it and their father took his truck to Amarillo and the other family he'd started. When Maggie went to bed, she put her hand on Sister's head like Sister used to do to her.

Sister broke the first and second rules two nights later when she dipped into her emergency bag and went into the bedroom of Maggie's eldest at one a.m. to tell her that Uncle Bo was shit for what he done and to always watch out for country songs and nice arms attached to big shoulders. Maggie came in while she was still crying and Maggie's eldest kept saying, "It's all right, Aunt Sis."

Maggie knew what it meant to send her back to Tahlequah. Ricky was away, but he was never far. She knew she'd get a call sometime over the next years while she was taking the girls to cheer, on Christmas Eve putting a mini trampoline together, out at a work party for her husband. What she didn't know was it'd be Sister with the gun and that Sister would be right and that it still wouldn't matter.

ROSCOE

THE BIG ONE, Telly, held my Cutco to Roscoe's throat. Roscoe looked at me with his brown dumb eyes and licked Telly's hand. Telly switched the knife to his free hand and wiped the other on his leg. He pulled Roscoe's nape so tightly his eyes slanted, but this just made Roscoe lick harder.

"Have they hurt you, Mr. Swanville?"

"No. They're threatening to kill the dog."

The little one, Bob Feathers, said. "Get our money!"

"Mr. Swanville, everything will be OK."

"It's not even my dog."

I had come home from the bar and thrown Roscoe's mini green football in the backyard. I was drunkenly patting him on the couch, both of us watching *36th Chamber of Shaolin*, when Telly put his fist through my door window.

"He was supposed to have shit," Bob Feathers said. He was tiny, tweaky, with a neck tattoo that said 'FUN' in fiery cartoon letters. I'd seen him playing foosball at the bar.

"You're a professor. Where's your money?" Telly pulled back Roscoe's head. Roscoe's shaggy tail thumped the floor.

"Professors don't have money," I said.

"Computers, guns, credit cards. Quit fucking around."

"Please don't take my computer."

Telly's biceps flexed. He was a large square Indian. At the table next to us at the bar, he'd hit on the waitress and laughed a large happy laugh. He hadn't seemed like a bad guy.

"Please don't hurt him," I said. I loved dog-sitting Roscoe. I loved his goofy Swede of an owner. After breaking up with his girlfriend, he'd gotten the dog and she'd gotten his friends. He wasn't in a place to handle Roscoe getting killed.

Bob Feathers went through my house filling a pillowcase with DVDs, my external hard drive, a blazer. He came out of my bedroom holding a pocket pussy I'd gotten as a joke gift, though I'd tried it out. He shook it at me. "What the fuck?" he said. "Where is everything?"

The blanket Telly hung over my door jumped with police lights.

Telly let go of Roscoe and stood over me. His ECKO sweatshirt smelled like layers of cigarette. He took hold of my wrist and drew the knife across the back of my hand. It opened up. I tried not to look at the blood. I did scream. Roscoe laid his head on my lap. My cell rang.

"Mr. Swanville, are you all right?"

"I'm fine," I said, though it was pretty obviously a lie. "We're in the front room. I'm sitting in the chair by the TV."

Telly said, "Shut the fuck up."

"They just want the money and a car."

"Put me on the phone."

I handed Bob Feathers the phone. He put down the pillowcase and traded the pocket pussy for his gun. He listened, said, "We told you," then, "10 and a car," then, "I'll shoot this guy and his fucking dog. 20 minutes."

"It's not my dog."

Telly slapped me across the face so hard my teeth rang. Bob Feathers said, "It was nothing. 20 minutes!"

They waited on the couch. Bob Feathers rubbed his head with both hands. Telly smoked and stared at Roscoe. Roscoe lay over my feet and sighed. My hand bled everywhere. I didn't want them to hurt Roscoe because I didn't want to die.

"We need music," Bob Feathers said.

"Shut the fuck up." Telly stared at the dog. Roscoe had barked, chasing his tail when they broke in. Telly had tripped over him. Roscoe gave me the time to dial 911.

"They don't think we're serious," Telly said. Bob Feathers said, "Oh man, oh man," and rubbed his head double-time. Telly took the gun and gave Bob Feathers the knife. He walked towards me and Roscoe.

"Take my computer. You can have it. Take my car."

Telly led Roscoe by the collar to the door. "Call them," he said. "Time's up."

Something popped another of the door's windows, tore down the blanket, and exploded.

The cops left some of Bob Feathers on my wall. Telly bled on my floor and grunted as the EMTs arrived. Roscoe, scared by the noise, hid under my bed.

I stood over Telly and said, "You don't hurt dogs. You don't hurt dogs."

LORD GAVE ME A MOUNTAIN

for Brett

HE WOULD HAVE WANTED me to have just that. It means nothing to you, Rey. I've got a guy can get any reel in the Oklahoma Hall of Fame. Masters, I know where, big names. It doesn't have to be this way. Rey, it can be good for all of us.

The kicker is . . . my dad was a mean son of a bitch. You seen that enough to know. I was the only one in the family who played. I'd filled in on drums the two nights he opened for B.J. Thomas, "Raindrops Keep Falling on My Head," right when everyone was crazy for Butch and Sundance. It was at the Muskogee Civic Center after Merle recorded "Okie from Muskogee." Big names came to say they played it.

I was 15, just looking for a place to smoke. I went up under the ramp where the bands set up. I was smoking and these three women come up over the ramp, big wobbly gals push right past saying, 'There he is!' Pulling out their cameras. I thought they was going for B.J., but it was my dad. Them saying, 'Sing "Houston," Sam.' That's good as it gets, I think.

Now you come to Nashville with $10,000 say, 'I'm a Nashville recording artist.' Back then? Hold on a minute, Rey, don't act so goddamn hasty.

I'm sorry. I don't mean disrespect. Old dog's gonna bark. What I'm saying is anyone can be a Nashville musician now. Back then? My dad cut 50 records, four on the top-40. He loved Jim Reeves, sang just like him.

Gene Sullivan got the Kerr Sisters out of retirement. They came and sang at Bradley Studios. You know about the Bradleys, that little Quonset hut. These are your people here. That's where you got your hooks in.

Dad'd come to Nashville every vacation. Six kids and a wife? He couldn't tour. But Tulsa, Tahlequah? They say you can't be a star in your hometown but he gave it a try. Before I was 15 he introduced me to Leon McAuliffe, Wanda Jackson, Stringbean from *Hee Haw*, Johnny Cash. Conway Twitty played guitar for my dad. Wes Watkins said he slept on the studio floor when they were in the recording booth cutting "Houston," just hoping to be invited in. That's all I want. Let me take "Houston." It means nothing to you, Rey. You can tell me being here my give-a-shit pedal's broken. Let me go and take it home. You got what I have to give.

B-side's "On Highway Patrol." My dad OHP 30 years. 30 years. Had to bring a paycheck home, six kids. My great-grandfather was a Marshal for Judge Parker. The museum in Ft. Smith, the picture of the Marshal reunion? He's the one holding the reins. My grandfather was OSBI. Two uncles, one nephew, cops. Dad had it in his blood. He'd never have done what he did with you boys but for music.

I do mean something by it. I fucking do. I know you don't like cops. I know he wouldn't have liked me acting a thief either. He'd've beat my ass for it. Yeah, I know you will. Go ahead. I know you don't need permission but go ahead. I'll give your boys 60 seconds of hell and then they can tune me like a fiddle. At least they can try. Just let me take the record.

Now hold on a goddamn minute. You're a liar on that one. That's what I said. He never did that and he never would do that. He only drew his weapon the once. Administrative leave, the only time I saw him in daytime not wearing his uniform until after what he did for y'all. Cleared of all charges. He used to sit on the back of the porch and have me set up matchsticks on our fence, 100, 150 yards away. He'd sit with the thirty-aught and try to light the matches. You know, hit them just so they'd light. He didn't cut a record after '72. He didn't cut a record in Nashville after "Houston." It's a yellow pressing. There's only but a few out there. I wouldn't have done this to you if I could get it any other way.

Momma said it was your debt and all he paid for it killed him as much as the car. Reason you have what I don't. Now you fixing to take away more, take a finger. Take two. I don't play now anyhow but maybe for church. His favorite was gospel. He didn't want to sing "Highway Patrol" on the B-side. He wanted to sing "Lord, You Gave Me a Mountain."

THE GAME OF MARVELS

LESLEA GOT the idea from her pastor, who had a sermon called "Bless-ed in America." She used the term a lot. She had a big, handsome, square-headed husband in sales and two shaggy, square-headed boys in sports, and in that way we agreed she was fairly blessed. Just her use of the term, though, the volume, made us think something awful was also going on, like crippling debt or infidelity, or there was something awful about her, like what we saw was all there was.

The Game of Marvels wasn't really a game. You had to bring up one thing we all took for granted but would be marvelous to someone from the Dark Ages. If you couldn't, you had to drink. Our happy hour wasn't that sort of happy hour, but St. Francis had been awful that week, a disastrous system update, and we weren't all blessed at home. We all said we wouldn't drink too much, but you know.

Terry asked, "Can it be marvelous in a bad way?" Terry would stop conversation with anyone and call them a racist. She played in a very competitive kickball league. She referred to multiple things as "dick" or "ass"—things that were eaten, were got, were bad or not there at all. She had tattoos of a bison, a potato with a shamrock inside, and her son's name.

Leslea said, "What do you mean?"

"Like awesome, eye-melting. Like an elder god." Terry played D&D. During her long stories we imagined a room full of men with bad facial hair and multiple energy drinks.

"I guess." Leslea said. We knew what that meant. She spared no judgment behind our backs, cupcakes to spouses. The thing is, we'd seen Leslea pass a homeless woman and then disappear. Apparently, she put her own coat on the woman and took her to a shelter. It was John 3:16 Mission she took her to, of course, but she never said anything. Only a couple of us noticed as she peeled off. It was Terry who told us.

The first marvel was cell phones, but Leslea said no, everyone knew they were incredible. People talked about them all the time. It had to be a totally normal thing.

The air conditioning kicked on, sending ripples in the fine hairs of our arms. A hipster couple opened the door and a quick, fat burst of hot air came inside. The sun had set but the asphalt held the boiling heat of the day. Most of us were on round two. Young ginger men in pink shorts walked by, oblivious. Everyone seemed to have agreed it was that type of night.

We all had ideas about marvels, but everyone shook their heads and smiled and said, "I just don't know." We drank in sips and wore blank expressions. Leslea sensed disaster.

Terry, who claimed to have been in a socialist screamo band in college, said, "Like clementines available in boxes year-round for six bucks."

Leslea beamed. A deluge of marvels arrived: salt and pepper at every table, streetlights, the interlibrary loan system, hand sanitizer, sunscreen, Tylenol, Febreze, disposable cameras, the progression from radio-network TV-cable-VHS-DVD-streaming, drive-thru cookie dough ice cream at Braum's, sedation dentistry. When one of us said Imodium A-D, Terry said that was the best answer yet, honestly.

There were things deemed too significant to count: the domestication of the dog, the Postal Service, pharmacies, the internet, GPS, the appeals court, the morning-after pill, the peaceful transfer of power after an election.

Terry tried to create a variant where we listed things that were perfectly normal now, but would seem barbaric in the future, like cancer treatment, but we enjoyed the Game of Marvels. Terry said her Magic

Wand and Leslea asked if that was a Harry Potter thing, then blushed when she figured it out, then said Harry Potter, especially at Christmas.

We fell silent. Some of us steeped in the impossible joy of snow. Some steeped in margaritas. For one group the distant chime of the holidays reminded us of home and waiting kids and god knows what Tyler or Cody got for dinner. For others, it was the long stretching quiet of the apartment, maybe delivery Thai, maybe booty call. For some, Christmas didn't recall home.

Leslea said, "The one I keep in my pocket is mortgages. It's such a simple thing but imagine being in the Middle Ages. Imagine trying to get your own land. And they just hand them out to you as long as you work at your job and keep things in shape."

Terry said, "Moist towlettes."

We all settled up and we all tipped well. The goodbyes took forever until, suddenly, large swaths disappeared into white SUVs and I found myself alone. I had a little walk. It felt good to walk a bit tipsy, the cool finally settling in. It was stupid enough that I didn't tell anyone. They'd think it was dangerous.

I skirted past empty Guthrie Green. I knew what waited at home. I knew the midnight treatment was coming. Jasen had done it drunk before. I could do it drunk now. She wouldn't notice, my poor girl. She'd be fighting.

I went past the Drillers stadium. In the distance, in front of the yoga studio, I could see my car. A group of young guys, three of them, walked across the street in the opposite direction. Two had on Cowboy orange, all frat boys, never a marvel, never welcome. One hung back, looking at me, then the other two slowed down. Greenwood was empty besides them and me. I thought: the car—too big. Pepper spray—too small. The key fob with a red emergency button in the center—a marvel.

LANDSCAPE WITH HOLE

Lately it's two walks a day. When it's dry, I walk the culvert by the elementary school up through the prefab mansions by Calvary Assembly of God. Second walk is down through the deserted dorms on the eastern side of campus. It's springtime.

They're cutting a new path along the lower part of the creek. Tahlequah tries to make things functional in small hopeful ways. The path runs by a sandless playground with a flaking half geodesic dome, by a house with a "FREE" bin offering wet children's shirts and a naked troll doll. The house spills out under a tin carport, a heavy bag and kitchen furniture piled with boxes. Walking on this new path next to the creek, I see a hole bored deep at the base of the rock hill.

The hill runs forty feet upwards at points, never steeper than right there, a rock wall. The hillside is covered in oak and Bradford pear and Chinese privet. I've never seen the hole before. It has a moldy crocheted pink pillow at its entrance. The hole looks like it's exhaling.

I'd been in caves during better times: at Devil's Den while an old friend visited, before Oklahoma. We bought cheap handheld flashlights. We descended holding the flashlights in one hand, keeping balance with the other. Dotting the walls at various points were little brown and gray sleeping bats. This was before they grew white fungus on their noses, disturbing them so they couldn't hibernate and starved or flew and froze, before they closed the caves.

We got to a narrow uneven point where we needed to stoop. Turning off our flashlights the dark was profound and oppressive. Our lights were so cheap. We were surrounded by sharp rock.

I hurry home, but what can I say about the hole? There was a lot to take in. No one was handling. I got queasy looking at screens so much. One morning it got so bad I wrapped myself in a blanket on the couch and shook uncontrollably. It's not like I could do anything but walk once or twice a day.

I go to find the hole, but I can't. Maybe it wasn't much of anything at all. I've had a few coworkers come to Tahlequah and become friends. They left for various reasons, one reason being Tahlequah. "The isolation was a killer," one said.

There's a sidewalk at the top of the hill. It's new too, with the fanciest streetlamps in Tahlequah. Half of the sidewalk is unlit, and half the streetlights are perpetually off, but it looks fresh.

The path below is black pebbled asphalt. The graded ground ahead of where they'd paved feels illicit, like eminent domain. The path butts against the unmowed backyards and fenced front yards of trailers. I see tweakers swinging their manic arms. I see sweating bearded men riding bikes trailing child carriers full of their possessions. I wear baggy linen pants and turquoise sunglasses some student left in a classroom. I am ridiculous, I know.

There's a phenomenon, widespread with teachers and students, called impostor syndrome. No matter how qualified or capable, you believe you're a transparent fraud. I feel this way constantly. In the classroom, in the bars, when I open my mouth and every clunky accent comes out. I did not catch impostor syndrome here, but it has metastasized.

The idea of the cave is obvious, I know. Tahlequah isn't the ideal cast somewhere in there. I don't consider Tahlequah the projection of a more ideal town. I don't consider any part of the town too risky, though you hear things. A man once came to my door at four a.m. and asked for a drink. I know these men need a way to walk from one place to the next as much as anyone, maybe more. The town is grudging towards them. I know Oklahoma blames people who can't take care of themselves. They pass the hole. They may sleep in it. I don't know.

There are elements in this town like carcinogens: everything is literal; there are pocket cruelties, apathies and disenfranchisements; distrust is general. There is a liquor store on every road out of town. The hole isn't some undercurrent of the repressed or the damage repression wreaks on repressed and repressor alike. The fact I can't find it discomfits me, because I am sure it's there. To just head the idea off at the pass, it wasn't a yonic thing either.

I find the hole. It seems like it could have been drilled for drainage. It has a natural look, worn out by water. It is like a mouth with the absence of a speech balloon. There is a camouflage folding chair washed down to the hole's front.

Things are worse, but it's hard to prove. I see the wiry tweakers but not the same ones. I see men shambling with women or alone. The kids have this crippling anxiety and I can't blame them. I've had four students break into tears this week. The threatening disasters that hover above them have begun to collapse. Cars rammed overnight. Chronic flareups. Derelict loved ones. A lack. I can tell they're living on their beds. I can tell they haven't been outside.

I find the hole again. It's near the base of a tiny waterfall that drops into a blue pool. It's opposite an L-bend in the shore. There's a concrete wall sitting in the middle of the wild grasses covered in a stutter of graffiti. At some point, a structure stood here, but it's absent. The scene is lovely except for the hole. It has a burger bag and shake cup from Del Rancho in front of it.

Last summer, there were signs warning of E. coli in the creek. Do not play. Do not drink. In the pool by the hole, a guy let his kids swim. Two skaters headed to the skate park yelled it wasn't safe. The guy thought they were mouthing him. He said he'd beat their ass.

There are caves in movies. The pathway to Mount Doom where Shelob lives. The hillside exit point in the false ending of *The Descent*. The exploding exhaust tunnel that Dash and Violet run from. The trauma caves of the many Batmen. The asteroid cave in *Empire Strikes Back* that was one long throat. The Fratellis close on the Goonies. Gandalf falls with the Balrog. There was the movie *The Cave*, but I never saw it.

The characters always find solace at the beginning. They've been hunted. They find a cave to sleep in. They go in for fun, to complete the mission, to find themselves. At some point, even if they're wandering near each other with flashlights, the characters stand alone. The cave becomes a place for horror.

Back past Shawnee where I lived in concrete, where someone cut the screens to get inside, where a man with big knuckles and a harrowed face asked if he could just come in for a drink, there's a grease-covered flock of men surrounded by parts outside Hoover Tires. There's a narrow metal footbridge to a bare stone path that leads to Bluff St. above. A pale man sits at a distance from a blonde woman with country teeth. They lean towards each other. There are trailers that look like fancy reclaimed cargo containers. The skate park is an ecosystem of teens. I've got no context for the landscape. It's a foreign place where I'm constantly wrong.

I go to the limit of the path, where the bulldozer sits. The new unpaved path goes under the tall bridge at Fourth. It's serene down here—an actual creek spilling prettily over flat rocks. I look up to the narrow eave where under-the-bridge meets the bridge. There's a man, motionless, wrapped in a gray sleeping bag. The path looks to keep going to Low Bottom, the dump, and past Tomcat Liquors to the south side of town.

Down there at the end, I give wide berth, ten feet easy, to an old man walking an old dog. I smile at him, like I do with everyone, as if it were a defense. It's the cheapest sort of optimism. He doesn't smile back. I detour down between the machine shops and the few tucked trailers off the path. There's a hypodermic on the ground. There's a replica rocket and broken glass outside the VFW. When I return to the path, past the hole, I come upon the old man with his dog directly ahead. If I speed up, it will look like I'm chasing him. If I slow down, I'll be in his wake. I can't get close, I know. He sees me and stares. I look like a threat. There's a second hole behind him, a bigger one. I'd never seen it before. Fallen trees lay across the opening. The old man and I are outside it.

IN THE BASEMENT

ONE EVENING, Myranda found herself following a man who had grown a new tooth by eating shark cartilage. Life had become intolerable—radiology desk, five tongue tacos from Jose's Mini Video, four-to-six Marlboro Lights, *Outlander*. At this point, she dreaded the cigarettes right up to the point she craved one, then resented it once it was lit. Sitting on her sister-in-law's hand-me-down couch—the couch Myranda said swallowed souls as if this excused falling asleep pajama bottomless with a mixing bowl of pasta on her chest—she stared at the email from the editor at the *Tahlequah Daily Press*. It encouraged her to 'find the parts of town that everyone loves but no one knows.'

"I felt the bump under my gums a month after I started taking the pills. I get them from Hawaii. Came in sharp as a razor. The science is out on it." The man was pouchy, goateed, titanically confident. Myranda noted in her phone that he had 'the face of a pontoon boater,' a notion compounded by his Hawaiian shirt, perhaps bought with the shark pills.

She told him she was a reporter and he said, "Strictly off-the-record," then told her at his house, just a short walk away, he had a wolf spider the size of a dinner plate he'd taught to hunt vermin. After two more beers, he confessed in whisper to a massive machine in his basement. "Wondrous," he said. "Maybe apocalyptic. Only of its kind in Tahlequah and eastern Oklahoma if not the world. I don't tell people."

He led her down College to Choctaw, then a little road by the transformer station. All the while he kept up the chatter, "You should know Greg is a bit of a recluse. Not the deadly sort, mind you. I mean he's a hermit. Not like the crab, I mean he prefers the company of himself, like many of us do. I make no promises. He's a spider. They're famously surly."

Arriving at the house, Myranda realized she didn't know the man's name. She knew he didn't have a job, a fact he pinned on the local economy, which was valid. She knew he once lived in Detroit. Everyone in the bar acted like they knew him, though in hindsight it might've mostly been the bartender. Myranda had been too interested in tooth, then spider and machine.

The house was a ranch like every house in Tahlequah. It sat rectangular at the front and ran back beyond where she could see. The man opened the door and started snapping his fingers past the dark doorway in a four-beat and whistling. Myranda had dealt with many many men she'd rather not have. This goateed, pot-bellied, shark-toothed, whistling, nameless specimen didn't concern her. She liked having a pretext for doing something dumb.

The man's snapping continued down the hallway. With his other hand, he fished a cigarette box out of his trousers and emptied one into his mouth. He talked the entire time. "You can see where he's been," he kicked by a powdery circle, a little ghost of unsettling diameter. "He's probably sluggish from laying around all day. Can you hear that?"

Myranda thought she heard a sweet, hungry sound like fire. She smelled the man's cigarette and the smell made her desire one, a genuine desire. Through the smoke they went past the bathroom into a series of hallways lined with moving boxes sagging into themselves. The man pointed out a biography of Robert Moses, a jersey from when the college's mascot was the Redmen, a set of St. Pauli Girl steins. Myranda made a note: "Moses. Boob goblets. Racist mascot. Eldritch air." Doors sat darkened perpendicular to further doors.

Myranda saw two long thin extensions of shadow peel from the floor up the doorframe into the hallway at her. She couldn't avoid flinching. The man said, "There's the boy!" She considered that she had done exceedingly well in finding an aspect of Tahlequah nobody knew and exceedingly poorly in finding one everyone loved.

He snapped faster, going into the door with the shadow following midway up the wall behind. The wallpaper was a brown terrible shade of green. The man stood at a sink peeling the red top off a yellowed tub of Marshmallow Fluff. He spread whatever was in the tub on his forearm. At his feet, a massive furred spider with black stripes like villainous eyebrows cocked its bristling front legs at the man as if ready to spit poison on him.

It spiraled up his legs so quickly that Myranda couldn't follow until it balanced between the man's arm and face, mandibles wide with the glistening forearm between them. The man chuckled and, once the spider scuttered back to his feet, wiped his arm off. "He was starving. No vermin today for him! It's a liquefied protein slurry. Only feeds if he can wrap his legs around something living." The man nudged the spider in the abdomen with the toe of his boot, "What a dummy! Come on down and let me show you the machine. Want a smoke?" She did.

He opened a door and turned on a bare light, the man stumping down the stairs ahead and the spider behind towards her heels. When she got to the bottom, the man was smiling bashfully in front of her. A low inhaling filled the hallway behind him. The sound made her jaw ache. She salivated from the cigarette.

"I won't feed you PR, given your profession. I found the room looking for that sound. You hear it, right? Like the noise grinding teeth make in your own head? The doorway was full of dirt. I started with a pickaxe, then chisels, now toothbrushes and a damp cloth. I thought about selling it at one point or getting in touch with people from the college. Each idea I come up with feels like a big rejection. I think it could really mean something. You'll see. Be honest."

The basement was the sort of packed earth Myranda remembered from the basements of her youth in New Hampshire. They were always full of canned food you didn't want, an archetypal damp smell, and feathery millipedes with black patterns covering their legs. The bachelor must made her weary. A motion detector flicked on ahead.

"I haven't seen a basement around here like this," she said.

"Houses don't have them. This one's older than Oklahoma. How they got the machine down here is a whole separate, like, galaxy of fish."

"You didn't build it?"

The man looked at the ceiling, "Are you serious?" There were no doors until there was a door, down the moist hallway the sound of the spider whispering behind them as the motion sensors turned the lights off.

The machine was rooted to the floor with a series of clawed feet, though tiny pipes extended below the dirt. In the middle, a quandary of intestinal, ribbed tubes, crevices and valves of stone, and a disk like a large sundial towards the top slope. The machine reached up so the clearance of the ceiling was only the width of a child's shoulders. It had no pointed edges, even the claws ended in tiny concentric circles. The sundial had three divots running into tubes wending their way into the machine's belly. It was less a machine than the innards of a huge beast cast in dirt. Circles covered the skin of it.

"How old?" she asked.

"I don't know how to answer that."

"You should turn it on."

"I don't think it's particularly pleasant." The man rapidly snapped in a low tick and the spider moved around and around the dial.

"I want to see what it does."

"I don't want to know." The man snapped a little slower. "Do you? Maybe this was a mistake. All of it. You try so hard and look like a fool. You really want to turn it on? Would it make things better? Maybe. But for who? Can you hear that crunching?"

She could. It was an invitation. Let this machine fire its revelations and release its ferocities. She valued that above what this man wanted. These hungers were hers and the disappointments she was done bearing.

IRON SPOKE FREE HOLINESS CHURCH

MADISON WOKE me up at noon after her shift at Daylight Donuts. It was summer break for her but not me. I'd been fired from A2B for calling in a bomb threat. It was more I told the shift manager that Chance Jackson was going to school shoot us because once he'd told me I'd get a warning and that morning he texted me three water guns.

It was more also I told a woman stranded by her rental that her coverage didn't cover a tow in West Texas and then told her, "Fuck, dude, calm down," when she called me a parasite bitch..

Madison held her fists under my face. The left smelled like strawberry frosting and the right like a maple long john. "You got fired," she said. "We're going on a choose-your-own-adventure."

I chose maple and she said, "Berry, you're eternally wrong." Strawberry held Adderall. "Those are for now," she said. Maple held Xanax. "Those are for after." Then me and her ate gummies, 25 mg each.

We drove to Sparrow Hawk Mountain, getting breakfast pizza at Casey's to go with the gummies. All that plus the Adderall made my stomach feel like a rock tumbler. The clerks talked storms, the ones just passed and the ones coming. Highway 10 was the same way my family took to church. The trees came over us like a green fist.

Madison smiled and there was a small face like a pocket on her real face. I first saw the small face when Bro. Thomas finally lost it with me for asking unworthy questions and all his grandpa warmth died for good. He told me my tongue was a restless evil, full of deadly poison. The small face was contained in the cheek and part of the nose and one eye.

Outside the car at the foot of the trail, there was screaming above us. I welcomed my end in the violence of the sunlight, a creature built to tear my limbs from wet sockets. The air carried the fat weight of a storm. I'd known it my whole life but didn't know it then.

"That's a good sign," Madison said. "Hawk."

"Sure," I said. "Makes sense."

My life didn't have open days until I left home and Iron Spoke. I only had the one guide. I didn't want to fail Madison. Hiking behind, her hair a black sheet, I thought it was a glory to her and my heart chewed itself. She said she kept it long for some ancestor bullshit and also she liked putting it into twin French braids like a Targaryen. It wasn't that I desired her. I wanted to inhabit her skin alongside her, for us to be co-pilots.

She'd grown up in the cult right down the road, Camp Sparrow Hawk. At Iron Spoke, they said the founder was a witch who disappeared babies and worshipped peacocks. Madison said there were peacocks, no disappearing kids unless you counted those like her that bounced. Only she would get me out of this hike alive.

"We had energy vortexes that brought us quicker to enlightenment. We practiced the healing arts." She said to me that the worst was she'd never feel so much a part of anything ever again.

In Sis. Jean's classroom, I seen five Kid's Krusades themes: The Frontier, Under the Sea, Faithful Bible Investigators, Fun in the Son, and Our Green Planet. In the last one she talked about "the fragility of our interconnected world." Bro. Thomas said it "headed down a secular path." He thought the children would be best served by another teacher. A few years later, he called me the earth which beareth thorns and briers. His sweater always smelled like Werther's Originals. He gave me the first Christmas present I remembered, a doll whose eyes closed when you laid her down.

I never knew leaves could make so much noise. I couldn't tell where the forest's panic ended and mine started. Madison lent me her sunglasses when I went down on one knee with the sun beating on me, the air moist and heavy as bathroom carpet. "Look at this fucker," she said. It was a baby robin, spindly and hideous except for its pretty robin face with its white spectacles. "He's destined for lunch."

I didn't think I could make it. "Better go along without me." I considered myself the honorable fallen, a Civil War casualty.

"Better stop being a little bitch."

"I'm going to die from getting high," I said. "I'm going to be the first." My heart was a goldfish in dirty water. I imagined my service at Iron Spoke, those Proverbs 31 women talking so my mom could hear.

"You're not going to die. I'm going to push you off the cliff and you're going to become a baby bird."

"I'd still die," I said. "They can't fly. Look at that robin."

"You'll shapeshift. You'll be spectacular. Think X-Men or Harry Potter. No one knows their powers until they face the shit."

I envied how she assumed everyone knew Harry Potter and X-Men. She was raised by Wiccans, people who thought Jesus was a communist and not the man who whipped the moneychangers out of the temple. The sky blackened ahead of us. It was storm season, but Madison didn't care. The trail turned. I half wanted to call daddy and have him bring the truck and sit in the back listening to Maranatha! Praise Band on The Oasis. Madison had the Harry Potter Society at NSU, intramural volleyball. I had nothing but a call I could only make once.

The trees ground back and forth like teeth. The wind was wrong. To the left, the sun made a green soup of the sky. To the right, growing darkness. Ahead, Madison's long hair. She looked back at me, her face half light. Her eyes glowed in possession. I had been led here to die. I would burn.

"Come here," she said. She smiled with her long teeth. "Look."

Bro. Thomas said the land around Iron Spoke was Green Country, God's country, as America was God's country. Madison invited me to the edge. To the right, a wall cloud came obliterating all the light, glowing in such green that I could feel the mattress over my head in the bathtub with my mother praying. Below us, the Illinois flowed. "Look," Madison said, "You can see fish." The light glinted in gold shards, the spirit of God moving on the face of the waters.

Madison's face was radiant. Two forks of lightning shot to the trees in the long dark valley. She laughed, "We're going to get it." A gust caught us diagonally toward the lip and I took one step without thinking. Madison put a forearm like a padded iron bar against my stomach. "Your powers," she said smiling with all her mistakes between her teeth. "Let's find them."

LOW BOTTOM SKY

When the dump did burnings, it spread a fine orange silt across Low Bottom. The full moon glowed toxic behind it. The hobos camped under the overpass poured out waving their bandanas like bayonets. "Here's the thing, pal," Buddy said. "You come on my property when I'm not right and it's not my fault, pal. It's the Civil War."

Buddy's cousin put him up for security guarding the secret Google server in Pryor. He let the boss know when two cooling system guys came in chemtrailing meth like nail polish remover but lost the job for pissing on the side of a server building, filmed by a drone like an aggrieved bat. He didn't qualify for unemployment. He went back to Low Bottom, the creek thick with dead crawfish.

Buddy played *Medal of Honor* on a PS2 that hadn't abandoned him, Nazis still there for killing. Rylee's keychain with the bat still hung by the door, musking his every entrance and exit with nightshade and iron. She'd smashed a bottle by his face after he'd put just the tip in bareback. Her black ponytail swung like a curse. "You have a curse," she said. "I have heritage." Rylee grabbed his hair in her two sharp fists. "Stay," she said. She pulled his beard with her fingertips showing dominance.

Daytime made Low Bottom a swamp of regret. She wouldn't get out of bed. He stared across the soggy crabgrass and wild onion beyond the creek an outflow. No sky out front but the abandoned Dominos. Black vultures cruised, old men in ratty coats. Night gifted new mistakes. She flew at him. He drank forties of the Silver Bullet. They gripped each other's wrists on the edge of real harm.

At Ned's, she bit a girl's throat who'd bought him a Randy Savage, lighting the top of the shot so it glowed blue in witch fire. Rylee knew the girl, had blown out a knee on the girl's hard pick during a game in Kenwood. The girl from a black-fingered family, the type haunts your window stealing the breath of your children with a wide McDonalds straw. When the night air hit Buddy he smeared the blood around Rylee's mouth into a grin. She leapt on his back and dug her heels all the way to Low Bottom.

Without her, Buddy killed slung dogs that prowled from the dump, grown hungry by scraps, mean from roadside betrayal so his rending hands were the fulfillment of a promise. He'd been betrayed by family too.

His cousin came over. They vaped moon pie weed until it steamed roaches out the wall. His cousin had turned their family's shit legacy into a long deployment in Helmand. "They're taking it back," his cousin said. "Rylee's people should take notes." His cousin tried to run the poison out, moonlight 5ks, left a fifth of Kentucky Deluxe, told Buddy to take care that night.

Buddy tore the loading dock door like a gravity bong's tinfoil top. He bowed up his shaggy arms with Dinty Moore, Ginzo Ramen Bowls, Captain George Fishstix, D'Augustino Pizza Biteys, a six-pack of Mountain Holler. He speared a 7-Up cake with one long nail and woke up on the floor to the cat licking beef stew off his fingers.

Buddy bought a 30-rack and made a castle of empties to keep the waters out. Rylee posted a picture of her and Bradley Cox smiling at each other with their teeth showing, #nubaewhodis☺<3☺. The cloud cover rolled off the black sky beyond where Buddy would ever know better. He texted:

-Miss me yet

-#olbaewhofuckdat

-B a bitch k thnx

-Eat ☀ ur queer

He sent a series of pictures of them in sweatpants, drunk, on the river, running the woods. He texted:

-U shld cum over

Then:

-Whore

Then:

-u shld cum ovr

At Ned's he got turned from the door. He tore two fingers off the bouncer who he'd played pool with and dragged the wet ends in a trail down storefront windows. The cops didn't know what to do with him. They didn't have the right bullets. Go back to Low Bottom, they said. Burn trash. Get spayed. We don't need any more of you.

Well shit, Buddy knew that. He didn't want to be like this. He wanted to smell a baby blackeyed like Rylee with huge thighs like him, holding the boy up to the night sky saying, "Someday, this will all be yours."

THE LADIES AT THE ARMORY

In a long lull between voters, Lacey told about her son's pants ripping from belt to inseam, no underpants. "It happened at Chipotle in front of God and the police. I told that boy about getting seen at Chipotle but he bent down anyway."

The traffic through the Armory polling station had been unusual. Typically, the ladies saw a big morning rush of working people, then intermittent busloads of the elderly, and late strays from the college. They were all sons and daughters of Oklahoma, by blood or soil or chance, and they all took a ballot from the ladies. That was the rule.

The ladies ordered Dominos. Whispering in the empty room, Cathy blamed the quiet on the Turbinos outside, not violent but looking it. Lacey blamed the Voting Commission lurking at stations across the districts, heels ticking in the halls. Cathy and Lacey worried in the printing and ordering of their ballots: the Commission targeted Fresno for destruction, sent night raids to Houston, swallowed children whole. It was difficult to tell what was literal. Adele cut her ballots in silence.

They said at the Elks and the VFW that the ladies lived together in a cabin by the Illinois. The men said the ladies got drunk on Mad Housewife and danced wearing only flowers during the big full moons—Blue, Super, Hunter. The women called them dirty, barefooted. Inevitably one man said, "Yeah, but you can bet back in the day."

A young burly bantam boy, red headed with a spiky cross on his shirt, necklace, and bicep each, strode into the polling station and cast around, hands on hips, like he'd turned on the light expecting roaches or a pregnant teen. The ladies regarded him with wariness, pity, and a little hunger, except for Adele, who was cosmically unsurprised.

He said, "I need a light one." Cathy asked him to verify his address and he said, "Why?" Then, as if he was answering his own question, he said, "I was blank before. I'm light now." He seemed to be asserting something grand, but Cathy was arranging and Lacey busy inspecting the man's underwear as he cleared his biceps while getting out his wallet, which also had a cross.

The man fed his vote, looked around and said, "Sure seems quiet," as if this was how it should be.

After he left, Lacey said, "I wouldn't mind seeing his pants split."

Cathy laughed. Adele smiled. They noticed a shape at the door. The Voting Commission had sent them to training with a man Lacey said had "the ghost eyes." In a nasal voice that italicized often, he repeated that monitoring would be increased. He said the *tolerant* stances of previous Commissions no longer held. He said penalties would be *swift* and *merciless*.

The man at the door was old, red suspenders, blue jeans presumably covering beefy old briefs. The expression on his face disgusted. "Ladies," he said.

They verified his identity with Lacey saying, "Oh my," often. As she prepared the man's ballot, she asked if he'd been standing there long.

"I guess," he said.

Lacey blanched. Cathy fretted, listed: all was in order. The man sat to his light ballot with the intensity of an accountant. The ladies sat in silence until he'd filled his boxes. When finished, he gave them a sour look.

"He's going to call the Voting Commission," Lacey said. She was near tears, but that wasn't new. They'd never been reported before, but it only took the once.

"They're going to burn us at the stake," Adele said. She was right.

THE LAST GREAT WHITE

When Ron saw the headline from his daughter, "Last Great White Dies," he almost picked up the phone. His daughter made a lot of noise for extinctions. Her posts had videos like the Oscars when they showed the dead. The animal as a kid; the animal surviving; the animal mating; the alpha; the carcass.

As a Designated Helper, he was only allowed to talk about store matters. Everyone on his shift was a college kid, except Alice, who asked him for drinks once then never spoke to him again, and Jimmy, who lost a wife to pills and didn't talk much. He heard one kid say to another, "Now I can swim again," and laugh.

Ron's whole generation got fucked by *Jaws*. Even in Muskogee, a 1000 miles from the risen Atlantic, something mean and refined waited in the lake. In sixth grade he wrote a seven-page science paper, longest he'd ever write. Most shark attacks happen in three feet of water. The bull shark goes up the Mississippi far as Illinois. The first great white was 50 feet long and killed everything in the old ocean. His daughter grew up on the lake. Now she lived by the Pacific.

She'd once asked his bucket list. At first, he thought his death row meal, like from the show: chicken-fried chicken with white gravy, mashed potatoes, a banana milkshake from Del Rancho. Then he got into it: seats behind home plate at InBev for a Cardinals World Series clinch; a fully loaded Ford F-1250 Super Duty; a night with Jennifer Lawrence. His daughter said, "Ew, god, nope." Then he said: go in a shark cage. And his daughter laughed.

He was late to work again. His manager threatened him with a final strike. He'd had inappropriate dialogue with another customer. A little black kid had come in with a great white t-shirt. Ron said, "You heard? You heard?" The boy's mother pulled him away.

He rented *Jaws* and *Jaws II*, *Jaws III*, *Jaws: The Revenge*, the *Jaws* reboot, *Deep Blue Sea, The Shallows, The Frenzy, The Open Boat.* Twelve High Lifes deep untying the Wolverines he still wore, he'd think, *the last great white is dead,* and a stale black cloud passed through him.

Ashing into the empties crowding under the yellow light of his kitchen, he read again the shark monitor's last reading: Thursday, 10:52. His daughter, a 1000 miles away by the dead Pacific, called his doublewide "the Muskogee swing pad." She said the guy she dated was "Armenian." They'd bred great whites in a lab but weren't close to release. Ron considered them frauds. The last great white died off the coast of Chatham. Its name was Bert.

He took a cooler to the lake, a chair, his gun. A fat old man alone in a lawn chair surrounded by young mothers with savage kids and packs of thuggish teens. He took off his shirt and drank four beers, his koozie wrapped in a paper bag. His belly was bloated and gray like roadkill. He waded past the kids and teens, out where pockets of cold gripped his toes. The kids scattered. He held his hand high, gun dry and shining. His daughter on a distant shore.

His father once took the family to Maine, farther than Ron could ever afford taking his own daughter. It was after *Jaws*. His father dared him to come in, swinging Ron's screaming sister over the waves. Ron watched miles of black water rolling towards him. The tide coming in. He made it to his knees. Shadows moved under the water, past the breakers, patrolling.

He treaded water in the lake, hand high, his daughter on a dirty distant shore. The swish of tail like a sword, fins like teeth on the surface of the water. A slow circle around him, a silent dive. He looked down and the murk of the lake receded past the emerald-gold sparks of the waterbound sun. A great swell under his feet, the gray snout with the black slits, the huge black mouth with perfect, white, box cutter teeth. The black eye, like a doll's eye.

AND THE CREEK

Shayanne smelled spoiled milk everywhere. The rain kept on enough the power wasn't coming back, but she didn't light a candle in case she fell asleep. Neesy squirmed and shrilled at the noise, her big cheeks deep red. Every bit of color on Neesy came from Shayanne. Neither got their color from Lisa. Shayanne's mom was pale where Shayanne was dark, had thin hair where Shayanne's was a rope. Lisa said Shayanne's hair would get thin now she'd had the baby.

Her battery at 7%, Shayanne watched on Facebook as red and orange bands looped over Ft. Gibson past Muskogee on the way to Hulbert and Tahlequah on the radar. She heard Travis Meyer say to seek shelter. Rain shook the trees and shuddered the trailer. She once went to Muskogee with her Granny Jean to see the USS Batfish. She remembered looking up the steep steps at her grandmother's support hose. The submarine was a dark hole. For weeks she dreamed it sank with them inside.

Yesterday afternoon as Shayanne stepped careful through thigh deep muddy water they sounded the siren. A fat twig coated in green little beetles bumped past her backpack. She thought of them climbing off the stick into the pockets, along the zipper teeth, out into the house at night. Little green living dots on her baby's lip.

On her last shift at Subway, no one come in from all the rain. Both Wade brothers mopped the doorway as water leaked in. Shayanne'd kept her hands in thin plastic gloves. Lisa used to take her to Hays Creek, barefoot where the water washed the stone slippery with moss. Now she said keep away. The Tyson chicken houses made the creek smell, water all cloudy. Lisa didn't trust any of it. The Wade brothers pushed all that brown water and Shayanne kept her hands dry making two footlongs with cookies for the next few days.

The little trailer kind of leaned on the edge of the property. Shayanne back from work wet up to her belt from crossing three flooded roads, including the county road came past their house. Wet down her back too from the rain opening up again. They exchanged Neesy in the dark, Shayanne smelling like mayonnaise and Lisa like sour milk and menthol. Lisa said watch the storms.

When Shayanne'd opened the door, the trailer was dark and hot. Lisa held the baby against her chest, her mother awake and patting her daughter's sleeping back. Lisa said she'd call and check on them if it got nasty. Charge your phone she said. If it gets bad come up the house. The creek shouldn't be anywhere near here. The river wasn't close. But the fields had got slowly swallowed up, ponds linking up with ponds and culverts so full you couldn't see where not to step.

In high school, Shayanne got the call to come fetch Lisa an hour away in Salina, where Shayanne had once gone to the racetrack. The police found Lisa holding her shoes by the roadside and called family until Uncle Jay told Shayanne to go on get her. Lisa wore a big man's t-shirt and had her hair swept over her face. She demanded they stop at Pig-N-Out, where she got a dipped cone with the change in Shayanne's cupholder and then spilled ice cream all on herself. Shayanne pulled over so her mother could cry. She parked in a lot on the side of Lake Hudson surrounding all of Salina and watched a big storm roll towards the town. She thought it would hit them straight on. She thought Salina would get swallowed by the lake, but Lisa kept on crying.

Shayanne could hear the sirens from the trailer, though she hadn't heard one today. She expected Lisa was keeping Granny Jean and Papa comfortable and then maybe come down to check on her and the baby. Before, Shayanne couldn't imagine sleeping in this, but being old might be like how she was now, forever tired, sleep ready to drag you under anytime, the day like constantly waking up. Neesy set to crying when the wind dragged a branch across the roof and she wouldn't stop. The trailer rocked in the dark, the rain constant against the metal siding.

In the nursing recliner, Shayanne fed Neesy and that quieted her some. There were tornado warnings every summer, a few coming pretty close. Lisa'd kept her in the tub in the shitty apartment in Tulsa when they was there. Shayanne remembered the few times Lisa had stayed out drinking or whatever, being in that tub alone under the sirens.

Then her and Lisa hiding in the closet with Granny Jean when Granny Jean made Lisa come home and quit drinking and carrying on. The closet smelled like her granny's sock drawer. It was nice and the storm passed right by. Shayanne remembered the sounds of the wind and three of them waiting. Lisa got mad at the storms and got mad at Shayanne as if the storms could hear them. The trailer rocked again. Now she was the big one.

Shayanne got angry at her mother for not coming down and caring more, even in a storm. The wind blew water under the door. Shayanne got a feeling for just how dark it was. She waited for a knock or the door just to open right up.

TWO GLASSES

DR. ENGLE SAID I could take anything from the garage pile. It felt like another test, so I chose the huge gilt mirror and four crystal port glasses. Engle had advised my thesis, "Foucault in Azkaban: Punishment, Authority, and Redemption in YA." He brewed and smithed, had four sons under ten, moved a heavy dresser solo in sandals, sported a Gondor beard, couldn't help with a job. "The thing about the mirror," he said. "It's a little cursed."

"Like, magically?" Maggie said the light in the bathroom mirror made her haggard. She'd said it more than once.

"Perhaps. It occasionally shows a reflection of the future. We think it might also show one's fears. Lily once saw herself choking out Little Seamus and that hasn't happened yet. As curses go, it seems fairly mild. Now these," he picked up a glass. "We didn't use often. Who drinks port? But they're enchanted."

"Enchanted how?"

"Whatever you're drinking tastes like itself, only more so. I drank a whole bottle of Oban with these. Massive peat, tedious refilling."

I lugged the mirror up the stairs to our apartment. Maggie was on the couch in footie pajamas, resplendent as a lioness. "Look what I got!" I hoped to win her over before dropping the curse.

Maggie stared into it, "God, I look haggard." Then I showed her the port glasses wrapped in sheets of the *Tahlequah Daily Press* and used student blue books. "Ooh," she said. "Those are pretty."

Maggie got home from A2B, another six hours of constant abuse from people panicking roadside by their Hertzes. Her job had no benefits, office bedbugs, a guy who displayed classic shooter tendencies. I'd called in to work because I couldn't stand one more minute under fluorescents with Mariah Carey yodeling at me, so I was already drunk.

Maggie called me Judas, her longest mistake, then declared her intention to also get wasted. That night we split a Four Loko I'd kept since senior year and, like everything about college, was fading and sour. I threw up in the sink while she cried on the floor, asking if this was it. The port glasses were a poor choice. She cursed violently from the hallway where we kept the mirror, because it sometimes showed things you didn't need to see while you were in bed and the hands started to wandering.

In the reflection was her image mixed with her mother's. I didn't show up, probably a blessing. "There are worse futures," I said.

"Name one."

That January it snowed in a way we hadn't seen in years. We couldn't afford to lose the work, but work decided for us. Maggie lay on the floor, looked at her phone and grew despondent. One of her sorority sisters had moved to France. "Please," she said. "I know it's ridiculous, but please take me somewhere soon. Muskogee, I don't care."

I had her get her scarf and boots on. Maggie's thick black hair spilled out from under her hat and around her gray eyes. I tucked the bottom of her scarf into her jacket and pocketed a flask full of Rumple Minz. Like German nobility, we struck out and like Dickensian orphans we arrived at the grocery store. We got Swiss Miss with marshmallows, two steaks, frozen crinkle cut fries, and a box of toaster strudel.

Bellies glowing, feet thawed, Maggie's face rosy as a young Mrs. Claus, we made the cocoa and drank from the port glasses. It was every post-sledding kitchen warmth. It was recess' end before winter break when Mrs. Galloway made it for the whole class. It was Maggie's grandmother and quilts from the back of the closet. It was red-fingered Finals Week snowball fights. The port glasses held two marshmallows. Each a balloon of hope.

Maggie saw herself wearing a call center headset, me potbellied and pajamaed in the background. She saw herself waking up and waking up and waking up. I tried to check my hair as the mirror showed it receding. It showed us together. It showed us alone. It showed us with other people, people we knew, which led to phone checking and other paranoias. We couldn't tell what was future and what was the other person's fear. So many of them showed me fatter. So many showed Maggie the same. I couldn't get rid of it. It had been a gift. "Why can't it show us something better?" she said, staring at my stomach.

"I don't think it works that way."

She took this as a comment on us. First, she started ducking her head in the hallway. Then she took to sitting on the far end of the couch wrapped tightly in her *P.S. I Love You* blanket. She'd come home from work, see me on the floor with a book, and shudder in a way that meant she'd seen this before.

I poured her filtered water in the port glasses, the taste like a cell regenerating. I kept refilling and refilling, standing her in front of the mirror.

"Look," I said.

She couldn't bear the sight. I kept looking for the both of us.

FENDER, CADDY, FINN, FENDER

When we bought the dog, he was Fender. The breeder, in apathy, advertised puppies Axle, Dipstick, and Shaft II. My sisters back east sent the money and I went south of Oklahoma City to Maysville. A hand painted sign in sky blue said "QT Terrier Kennels," the ground tired from the traffic of dogs.

Inside, the carpets were so marinated in urine they crunched. Concrete rooms of cages fronted by plastic tubs held shaking befuddled rags. Fender was in the presentation area, a putting green with a Little Tykes table and chairs surrounded by fence. He had the face of a wary old man, like I was trying to steal his meds.

I drove home with my hand covering his whole shuddering body. I took him out on the freezing grass at 2 in the morning with no leash just to see if he'd come back. His ears hung down at the tips and he slept in the crook of my arm. "Lil' Fucker," I said, and he bit the webbing of my thumb.

I lived in a house with laminate, industrial carpet, all brown everything. In six years, I'd housed only a kitten that showed up at my nighttime door with a leg torn to muscle. I saved its life and gave it away. You could count the roaches, the caterpillars, the millipedes, the sugar ants, a spider I named Franz that I confided in while flicking sugar ants at his web. "Well if it isn't Franz," I'd say over coffee. I lingered at the supermarket checkout, bewildered by basic etiquette. As I lay with my arms wide, Fender tried to bite the carpet while running and flipped clean over. He was scruffy as a hobo, prematurely balding as a hobo. We had things in common.

I took a picture of him looking up between two couch cushions with his inscrutable black eyes. He was every ounce the little shit. He bit my face. He jumped claw first on strangers. He pissed on the couch staring me right in the eye. There was a tangible likelihood he would become an asshole.

My sisters swooned from the east. My older sister, gifted in leading with her heart, thought he might save our father. My little sister, a jaguar of professional elegance but impatient with affection, asked for constant updates. I sent pictures of Fender peeing at 3 in the morning and they lost it. I sent pictures of him sleeping with dreaming paws extended in flight. They lost it.

On Christmas Day, my mother pretended to adore him. It was a new opportunity to prove such things. She's a wonderful mother, cooks soups and cries at airports. My father couldn't muster. He had a depression so ferocious his mind rode a tiny track around his failures. He still mourned Mack, his previous terrier who had swaggered like a seesaw. My father saw Fender and said, "I can't." My nephew came up with the name Caddy, because my dad loved golf. My mother didn't take to it. I saw, like the Ghost of Christmas Future, the mistake we'd made. In a haymaker attempt at connection, my mother named him Finn. Finn née Caddy née Fender mauled the low-hanging ornaments, all from our childhood.

Sometimes, alone here in Oklahoma, I wonder how I belong to my family. Growing up, I kicked my dog, Tam, for eating the nunchuks of Panthro the Thundercat. In second grade I organized a mob to beat a kid who had yellow braces and smelled like homemade peanut butter. I forget my nieces' birthday presents every year, so riddled with guilt that I guarantee missing the next birthday. I understood Finn wasn't a monster. We just weren't particularly great. At the airport my mother cried. Finn looked from the backseat window as his only link to home abandoned him.

My parents sent him to training. Now he wears a collar and they shock him by remote. My father got worse. Finn didn't cure him, of course—he's awful. My father tripped on him and exposed the bone in his shin. Now my mother has to care for three aliens: my father's depression, his weeping leg, and Finn. My little sister's apartment complex is fascist about dogs. My older sister's heart is weary from leading her children, our parents, her husband, her own dog that Finn tormented over Christmas.

I saw Finn in March, my parents housebound, overwhelmed by a late nor'easter. Sandy lunar formations covered the winter beach. For miles it was only the two of us and the surly ocean. I let him run off leash. He wouldn't go far before turning to wait for me, grinning. Then he'd run again. He ate something long dead but didn't get sick.

My house is freezing and brown. The laminate is cheap. The landlord lays down poison for everything. I keep terrible hours. I drink at 4 in the morning until Frank Ocean blares and I'm crying in my kitchen. I smoke on my couch with chocolate on my bare chest. I've lived so long alone I don't know if I'm meant for people. We wouldn't be good for each other. But if they can't love him, if he can stand me, if he could handle one more change, I'd say, "Fender, you little shit, let's go outside."

AT THE TRAIL OF TEARS EXHIBIT

The second time my parents came to Oklahoma, we went to the Trail of Tears Exhibit. My father, Boston Irish, second generation, altar boy, pharmacy night clerk to put himself through college, married five decades to my mother, described through my life as "a good shit."

My father, gifted in business and fathering, once a true genius in playing the right side between busting balls and cruelty, who did the polling for Jimmy Carter, pitched Eisner at Disney, ran damage control for Niagara Mohawk. My father, who taught me the world was my possibility and worked to make it so. My father, not a student of history.

He entered the Exhibit led by my mother, because, at this point, he needed some leading. He stopped by every placard, stockade testimonial, court document, military order of removal, artifact of survival, map with arrows going one direction, haggard mannequin, accounting of loss. Silent until we got outside, he said, "Jesus, the shit we did to them, huh?"

Later, I learned things about my father I wished I didn't know. I live in this town at the terminus of the Trail of Tears, capital of Cherokee Nation, another in a long pale line claiming suspect ownership. I've told that story of my father many times. First, as joke. And then as explanation. And then as apology. And then, and then, and then.

OH SILENT NIGHT

At the Help-in-Crisis Red Shoe Gala Planning Committee meeting, everyone stared at the television. Janey heard them saying how awful it was, asking how it could keep happening.

Ellen Schulman came to Janey and talked about LaDonna's hog fry. "The family was aghast I don't eat pork. Everything had pork. I'd wager dollars to donuts I'm the first Jew to step foot in the house. And they were absolutely lovely. LaDonna's grandmother made me chicken soup right on the spot." Janey loved Ellen because Ellen had been to Cinque Terre, wore pastel pantsuits, and stayed in Tahlequah.

They finalized the giving list. The owner of Mary's Liquor donated three bottles of pricey reds for the silent auction. Jill and all the folks at Tahlequah Health sponsored a block of tables. Steve and Sue of the Unitarian Universalists couldn't attend but gave what they could. Janey thought how kind all these people had been the past months. The casseroles they'd made. How they didn't ask when, like a cat, she stared at empty spaces.

At the Unitarian Universalist Church where Carl once sang "O Come, Emmanuel," Janey again had her arm squeezed, was offered hugs she didn't invite and didn't refuse. Around the room, arranged for the Arts Council's Winter Concert, people talked about how the world had changed. Ellen gripped her arm, "There are too many bitches here." Ellen had come to see if Becky Jane Fletcher would show her face.

Steve talked Unitarianism yet again to Janey. He said Buddhists, pagans and bruised Christians found fellowship here. Janey smiled politely, resisted. She saw faith as a gift others had, like charisma or diligence, something innate that carried you. Carl possessed it and it had illuminated his life. For years, it frustrated him to not share it with her, and Janey resented not having it. Going through the motions was somehow worse.

The Mandaphonics strummed through "O Tannenbaum" and "Have Yourself a Merry Little Christmas" on mandolins and lutes. In front of Janey, Ann Fite's mother clutched her weak winnowed hands. The Mandaphonics began "O Holy Night." Sunlight came low through the squares of blue glass, catching the faces of the audience in shining profile. "Fall on your knees. O hear the angel voices." A silhouetted woman began to softly cry. Janey recognized her hurt in the Quaker simplicity of the room, the battered wood of the floor, the smell of homemade hot chocolate.

She snuck out as soon as the program ended. Winter twilight closed in on her. She wrapped her scarf, cedar smelling, knit by a girl at the Help-in-Crisis shelter. Last April she had packed both their winter coats into bins with little cedar balls Carl sanded to keep fresh. She stood beside her car and thought of sitting in it waiting for the heat, of home and the sound of her breathing and relenting to the television. They'd cleared the street for something: Tahlequah's small Christmas parade.

A chatty party took up The Branch's dining area, no one Janey knew. A selection of couples huddled over their candles. No one sat at the high tables that overlooked the dark creek where Chekhov, their second yellow lab, once caught crawfish. Janey could see the start of the parade. The Tahlequah High marching band foolish, prideful, and sweet in their orange smocks.

The young mayor of the town in the bed of a Dodge Ram caught his young son teetering against the weight of his little jacket. Four wheelers with roll cages festooned in lights zigzagged like country Shriners. Children on their fathers' shoulders caught candy canes from doctors and nurses with their scrubs decorated in tinsel. Children pointed, giggling, at the sanitation truck with Snoopy painted on the side sitting on the toilet while their parents suppressed smiles.

At the bar, two men watched as the news reported horror in a school, a horror to families, a horror to children. Janey watched the shade of her reflection in the window. Outside, in pink and blue on a trailer with a giant Angel Tree, children sought donations for other children. Janey felt something crawl on the edge of her chin, found tears. She hated getting backed into ten-minute conversations in Reasors wearing sweatpants as she bought single potpies. She hated how Rani Ketcher got shunned from her church when she left her abusive husband. She hated that the women at her funeral here would never have known her when she was ferocious.

The Sequoyah High band marched past swinging their brass. A parent ran from the crowd and adjusted the listing hat of a tuba player, and a French horn player patted the tuba player's arm. A toddler dressed as a snowman peered directly at Janey over his mother's right shoulder. She had no answer for that look. She wiped her face.

At home, in the silence, she unbraided her hair. It was long and entirely gray, and she still loved letting it loose at night. It was strong hair. In the dresser mirror she watched her hands as they worked. Strong hands that didn't ache too much. Her nightgown smelled clean. She knew where the house ticked as it grew warm. This Halloween, a tiny girl in a fairy costume walked right in her front door. You could see Boyd Sixkiller's adopted family in his driveway hugging as they got out of their truck at Thanksgiving. The street was now full of electric candles in the windows.

In the shadow of the bedside lamp, Janey acknowledged Carl. She knew the shadows burned on her retina and the force of memory put him there. She knew this would end, but for now it didn't bother her. It was a comfort. A weary world rejoices.

BILL

When Bill tasted the ribs, they were real nice. He'd never set out to raise a boy who could build an engine or smoke meat, but he didn't avoid it, and the result was sitting on his plate covered in Head Country.

Bill's son, Buddy, and his granddaughter's husband, a big Cherokee fella worked on a road crew in Northwest Arkansas, were kicking ass in horseshoes. Bill put away his fifth rib as Bud capped a ringer and dropped another to advance to the quarterfinals. Bill'd been eliminated in the second round, but that was OK. He hadn't gone far in the tournament in a while, and it gave him time to eat his ribs.

Bill's wife of 47 years, Tammy, sat with a sweet tea laughing with her sister, Becky, up all the way from Brownsville. The two of them hated each other for years, some teenage grievance soured too long. Once, her sister told Tammy the whole family was counting down to the divorce, though Bill never imagined himself divorcing. Tammy said Becky'd know from Tony sleeping around and TJ beating her ass, and that probably took it too far. It was the wedding of Becky's son that brought them back together and ever since they were thick as thieves. Her sister knew how to get Tammy *drunk*.

She'd earned the sweet tea and the white zin to come. Next to the ribs she'd laid out two dozen deviled eggs, French onion dip in a little whipped peak in the middle of sweating cherry tomatoes and cucumber slices and broccoli crowns, barbecue beans made with brown sugar and mustard, potato salad with bacon bits, pickled okra and small bread-and-butters canned alongside jalapeno jelly and wild cherry jam; later, she'd bring out pineapple upside down cake as well as a plate of brownies.

She'd earned it sitting in her chair in shorts with her fan just laughing. This morning she'd been hard on herself, something Bill had long gotten used to though it was never easy. The kids kept themselves happy around the pool and the older ones took to their beers. In the house, two of his granddaughters held their babies in the dark of the AC. Another granddaughter played cornhole with her fiancé. The few clouds couldn't block the sun and it was hot everywhere, everyone headed toward sweaty and tired and drunk on beer. It was the 4th, that's all you had to say.

A red Chevy Avalanche came creeping down the road. It was goddamn Errol's. Bill knew his truck from the Facebook where every single thing his brother put up, from his dog wearing Oakley sunglasses to all the MAGA garbage to his kilt collection, had the same effect of wearing Bill out. The road had been graded last week, but his brother eased the truck gingerly on.

Tammy seen the truck and looked over at Bill, who shook his head. The last time Bill saw Errol, it'd been a different truck and Bill had his shotgun, though he'd never racked it or pointed it anywhere but the ground. He'd gotten the gun before he found it was Errol making all that noise in Bill's own kitchen at five in the morning. Errol with a sack half full of their momma's collection of shot glasses from everywhere their parents had traveled, mostly Arizona to Niagara Falls, and then a heavy dose of Europe their mom did with her church group. He'd had the shot glasses two weeks when he found Errol off the wagon and in his kitchen, had buried their mother two weeks before that.

Bill didn't love the shot glasses, but she'd left them especially to him. She'd left Errol her brother's antique license plates and her cast iron pan, until the end hoping he'd take up cooking. None of it was worth the cost of postage, but there Errol was, on a stepladder, wrapping each shot glass in the *Tahlequah Daily Press* and the gazette from St. Brigid's with a damned winter hat over his head and a doctor's mask on his face though it was September and 70 outside.

Errol left the glasses and Bill didn't raise the gun and Errol got in his truck and that was the last they'd seen of each other for nearly a decade, until Errol pulled into Bill's driveway with two paper bags of fireworks and his wife holding a red, white, and blue cake from Walmart.

It hadn't just been the shot glasses, though:

- Bill split Errol's eyebrow open with a detached bike handlebar (age 11);
- Errol told Ruth Panther, who the brothers had given shit to each other for liking, because they both liked her, because she was good looking, blond as the 4th of July and smarter than all 32 girls in Bill's class and, honestly, all 29 boys—and, it turned out, smarter than most everyone in Errol's class, too—that Bill still wet the bed, which ended up getting around to everyone so that Bill was called 'Spot' until they all went to high school and Bill fixed everyone's motorcycles and then bought his own, which changed opinion on him (ages 13-16);
- Errol borrowed Bill's Thunderbird, his first car and second vehicle after the motorcycle, loaned after Errol told him he was just going to get Andy Capps Hot Fries and a Dr. Pepper, stop being such a pussy, then wrapped it around a tree, which led to a brawl and 36 stitches between them (age 17);
- Bill didn't stick up for Errol when their father wouldn't loan him a few hundred bucks for an apartment and truck down payment, stayed silent when their father said the money would go to beer, the casino, and stupid women, and Errol said it would go to the damn job he'd just got at Bixler, the same sort of pipefitting work that brought Bill to oil & gas, which kept him for his entire life and allowed for this house and all the family around him, and their father said it didn't matter how much money Errol needed, he'd just piss it away, and through all of it, though Bill knew about the job and Errol trying hard to get it, he couldn't just once have his brother's back, and Errol pointed to this as the moment things went sideways, where he could have gotten his life on track but for Bill being a coward (age 26);
- Errol hit on Tammy at Thanksgiving, this about a month before his arrest (age 30);
- Bill had words about Errol messing with the grill (age 34).

And on and on for 20 years of grenades lobbed back and forth in threat, trespass, and bullshit, on either side, always heavier on Errol's side because he couldn't do right even in his best pants though Bill would never say that, not even when pressed, except to Tammy as they sat in bed at night and Bill was quiet and carrying regret to sleep.

Errol's wife, Bethanie, wearing a few American flags, moved away from Errol immediately, holding the cake like an offering. Bill didn't particularly favor her—Bethanie never let not knowing something get in the way of voicing her opinion—but she'd come at a time when Errol had just started drying out and putting things back together and seen him through the backsliding and rough moments after.

Errol stood watching the horseshoes, wearing crimson and cream same as always. He'd gained weight in his gut and carried more gray in his mustache. He didn't look bad. He had his hands dug into his pockets and followed his wife a few steps behind. Bill realized, however she'd gotten invited, it was Bethanie made him come.

Bill had seen Errol just this way before—at the only middle school dance Errol went to, at Bill's wedding where he was the last groomsman, at the Tahlequah Police station when Errol had to hit up Bill because their father was done with him.

He'd seen him the other way too, though. An older brother is always an older brother. Errol once could hit a straight fastball a clear mile. He could dance two-step with any woman and make her feel like something. If push came to shove and you needed it, he'd step to anyone in a bar fight, any size. When their father died, it was Errol carried the weight—the details, the bad news, the shaking hands—while Bill had it rough. There were things you couldn't repay on both sides and it didn't really matter much in the end who had the better argument.

There were things Bill would never think of but were also true: he knew the first and last name of every person in his yard by the pool and the barn where his granddaughter and her husband stayed so they could save up for a place of their own; by the house he'd put plumbing into, wiring he'd fixed, the carport he'd built; by the garden behind the pool he raised potatoes and tomatoes and asparagus that took three years to even start producing, surrounded by kinds vegetable, human, and vehicle that he grew, nurtured, and repaired, people he'd taken in when they didn't have an option and supported when he could; and in her chair in her shorts with her fan, just on the cusp of being ready for a glass of wine, his wife who had stuck with him when he was four months on a job and who'd fed every person here for decades, his wife who'd watched his foolish, drunken brother make a pass then laughed, patted Errol's back, and told him to get the hell to bed, his wife kept her eyes on him just to make sure he was all right with this arrival on his favorite holiday; and there was the fact that most everyone there would quit a job or move across state or cancel serious plans if he asked because he never did and if he had, it wouldn't have been for himself.

Buddy had recognized Errol by now, Uncle Errol, and Bud, half-drunk and funny in a way that Bill admired because he couldn't understand how it worked, went up and shook his hand and then looked over at Bill, at his dad. Just checking up. And after all that, seeing his son do it right and his wife making sure it was all right after all her good work and the rest of the family glowing around him, Bill got up to see his how his brother was doing.

TWO-STEP

I WATCH you dance with Shane in the big rodeo corral of Bar 918. It's oppressively country even for Oklahoma. Shane's six-foot-two, all Levi's and self-deprecation. You're something else. The lights alternate bar mitzvah orange and blue. You're two-stepping. We have plans to bird watch in our old age, mine sooner than yours.

You taught me two-step. Though there are only three steps, I constantly need relearning. You laugh whenever I dance. This pattern—forget, teach again—is a homey point of contention, like our couch. Of course, you're right: my dancing is a disaster.

Before, I asked Timmy Tiger where you and Little Ralphie went and he said, "We don't all keep track of each other." He said he meant Cherokees, like you, and I thought he meant gay guys, like Ralphie. Either way, he was laughing, and I felt like an ass. Timmy said two-stepping was the official dance of white people. I circled my face, gave him the 'not all white people' and he said I was the other kind, Sweater White. I rhymed yachts with square knots.

Earlier still, at a gluten-free brewery ringed by your art, you bragged on me karaoking Ludacris's verse from "Gossip Folks" by memory. There was a whole tangent on snagging, hooking up at powwows and such. The jokes were mild and strange. I come from a long line of "it's not offensive if it's funny," a long heritage of not-funny people. I watched out for jokes I didn't belong in. I'm still learning to pivot.

I often say you have a voice like a Disney princess, and you say, "I can't sing." It's like when I compliment your butt and you say, "I don't have a butt." Or like when I call you brilliant and you say, "I don't see why." It's the easiest thing in the world, telling you true things you refuse to believe. All night you're unimpressed, moving forward.

At the brewery, your bangs were kinetic. You said, "I love it!" when you saw things that delighted you: Alice's shawl, Timmy's tiny wine pouch, this group of people no longer strangers to me. Your back was an agony of nerves tucked against your spine from preparing for your show, but you animated the table. You talked about race cars and setting picks in basketball and spook trails. It's all become a language I've learned. You smiled with your chin thrust out.

We held hands walking down the street headed to a unicorn bar, the saddest place in Tulsa. I watched dudes malingering around the dance floor like carnies. The sight made my scalp itch to back when I was unsteady with hygiene, unsure of what to do with my mouth, leering at every wrong time, careless with what was given to me. At times I doubt what's left of my talent for reinvention.

Shane can two-step like he got it in church when he was eight. Shane I don't mind, though you look good together. I might be making a mistake, but at some point you have to be ready to look like a fool. I watch you step on beat, watch Shane spin you and smile. You grapevine, another move I can't master. I still think that I could learn. You quote *Beauty and the Beast* in Shane's handsome little ear, your black braid whipping, thick as the rope you'd throw a drowning dog.

JORDAN

From inside, Jordan watched Buster and Lucky Lou lay in the dirt driveway. Buster was barely past a puppy, but he made it farther than the last one. Lucky Lou had been hit by three cars, two he'd caught, had parvo bad, but Lucky Lou was Lucky Lou. Nothing was fair.

Jordan waited for Tiffany coming in her beater Trans Am. It was already her third car, Mr. Goingsnake selling one then getting something shittier. The last one, Tiffany had to tear open the door panel while she was driving and put out an electrical fire with her hands.

Jordan started crying when Tiffany had sent pictures of her burnt hands. She felt like a damn tittybaby. The fire happened on 82 heading south to Tahlequah. Tiffany's cousin, Makayla, was a freshman at NSU. Tiffany said the bouncer at Ned's, who'd had two fingers tore off, thought all Indians looked the same and let in any girls not too drunk to walk.

Jordan never went to Ned's or spent a night in a college dorm. Her mother'd beat her ass. Her dad would probably quote Bible verses at her now, but she thought he'd still get froggy and break something.

They didn't know about her sneaking out her bedroom window and riding with Tiffany at night when her dad wasn't in a patrol car. He was home by six, smoking alone in the garage, praying before bed. Jordan's dad had been first on the scene.

They'd head to Kum & Go and get slushies and Tiffany would pretend she liked cigarettes. They'd ride Rollercoaster Hill, Jordan telling Tiffany to slow down the whole time though it was Jordan made them come.

Last time, they went by the tree. Jordan felt where the trunk had splintered like torn stitches. Her classmates put up a big white cross and decorated it with a football jersey, plastic flowers, and photos ruined by the rain.

Blake had given a little metal decorative cross to her parents when his family came over in third grade. His mother said he'd seen it at the flea market. He'd also bought a small metal daisy he gave to Jordan between the parents in Jordan's living room. For two years Jordan hated him.

Jordan's parents thought she was going to the movies, but Tiffany was taking her to Tulsa. She wanted to take Jordan out to coffee though Jordan knew Tiffany didn't drink coffee. Jordan hadn't ever been to Tulsa alone. When she went with her parents—to Woodland Hills for back-to-school shopping, once to see a Drillers game—her father said you had to be careful. Her mother had stared down black kids cutting up.

Jordan hadn't gone over 65 more than a couple of times the past few months and the first time she begged her mom to pull over. Her mom said, "We need to drive." Her father told her mom to ease up for once.

Jordan didn't tell Tiffany when they went to the tree, hadn't told anyone, wouldn't have told Blake if it happened to someone else, it was like she'd been struck by lightning and split in two. The bark, the part everyone saw burnt and dead.

The other part stood in the dark with her hand on the splintered wood as the wind went through the leaves into the fields. In the far hill was the tiny light of a campfire. The wind felt like electricity that ran to every hair on her wrists to the tips of her teeth out into the big dark.

She saw Lucky Lou tear ass down the road, running back leaping next to the bumper of Tiffany's Trans Am. Buster and Lucky Lou scampered as Tiffany came in hot. With her burnt hands on the wheel, Tiffany smiled in the full sunshine. Jordan burst out the door going fast.

ACKNOWLEDGEMENTS

One of the joys of having a first book published is finally thanking the lifetime of people who helped make it possible. It's also daunting. I'll keep this brief and beg forgiveness from those I've foolishly overlooked.

For the teachers who encouraged me—from Doc Fast at BHS to Gabe Hudson, Ben Marcus, and Meredith Steinbach at Brown to Ellen Gilchrist, Molly Giles, and Skip Hays at Arkansas—you lit the way. Skip, in particular, was a mentor to me, as he was for so many, while I was at Arkansas and after.

A number of people read this manuscript or stories within it and gave me much needed feedback: Matt Goldberg, Steve Sanders, Amanda Bales, Jessica Cornell, and Nick Claro. Whether improving my craft or checking to make sure I represented Oklahoma correctly, thank you for your generosity and insight

So many people in Oklahoma have been paragons of the warmth, honesty, good humor, and patience that I associate with the state. Brett Fitzgerald is a true Green Country ambassador, proclaiming himself always as "just a redneck from Muskogee." The folks in the Arts Council of Tahlequah, and the many artists of Tahlequah, helped open the town to me. All my students, colleagues, and friends at NSU have given support, opportunity, and kinship. I count myself improbably fortunate that I was given the chance to teach here.

Perhaps no one has shown me more of this place and guided me through it than Kindra Swafford and her family. The Thilgeses in particular opened their home on so many occasions. Linda and John Thilges are the matriarch and patriarch of this place for me. While my work pales in comparison to Kindra's art, many of these stories would not have been possible without her.

Thanks to another inspiring local artist, Roy Boney, for the spectacular cover image. I don't know how many book covers I'll get, so I wanted my favorite bird on this one, and he obliged wonderfully.

Deep appreciation goes to my publisher, editor, and friend, Jeanetta Calhoun Mish. There is no greater advocate for the written word in Oklahoma on every level than her, accessible to all, speaking for all. My thanks also to Rilla Askew, Brandon Hobson, Skip Hays, and Ben Nickol, who honor me with their words.

Finally, and most importantly, my love and lifelong gratitude to my parents, my sisters, my nieces, my nephew, and my brothers-in-law. It was a cosmic stroke of good luck that I was born into my family, and I will forever be thankful for it.

ABOUT THE AUTHOR

Photo by Dalton Perse

Raised outside of Boston, Christopher Murphy attended Brown University and The University of Arkansas. He serves on the editorial board for Nimrod International Journal of Poetry and Prose, as well as the boards for the Arts Council of Tahlequah and the Oklahoma Humanities Council. His work has been published in *Gulf Coast* (online), *This Land, Jellyfish Review, Necessary Fiction, decomP, Spartan, Ghost Parachute* and *The Tulsa Voice* among others. Currently, he's an associate professor of English teaching creative writing at Northeastern State University.

www.ingramcontent.com/pod-product-compliance
Lightning Source LLC
LaVergne TN
LVHW010629100826
845148LV00014B/3173
* 9 7 8 1 7 3 2 3 9 3 5 9 2 *